Avram's Gift

Text © 2003 MB Publishing/Margie Blumberg
Illustrations © 2003 Laurie McGaw
Book design © 2003 PageWave Graphics

First published in the United States by
MB Publishing, LLC
7831 Woodmont Avenue, PMB #312
Bethesda, Maryland 20814
USA

First Edition
1 3 5 7 9 10 8 6 4 2

Library of Congress Control Number: 2003090250
Blumberg, Margie
Avram's Gift/ by Margie Blumberg; illustrations by Laurie McGaw — First edition
p. cm.

Summary: Mark is afraid of the photograph of his great-great-grandfather Avram from Russia. Who was Avram, and was he really as stern as he looks in that photograph? One special Rosh Hashanah, Mark learns the answers to these questions from his Grandpa Morris and discovers Avram's gift.

This is a work of fiction.

ISBN: 0-9624166-2-2 (acid-free paper)

Printed in Canada by Friesens

Avram's Gift

By Margie Blumberg
Illustrations by Laurie McGaw

MB PUBLISHING

In loving memory of my great-great-grandfather Avram Itzik
and my great-uncle Morris — Menashkeleh — who inspired this story.
And for all the other *eleh*'s in my life, with love.

MARGIE BLUMBERG

In memory of my grandfather
Jonathan Alexander Proctor,
who emigrated from Ireland with
an open mind and an independent spirit;
and to his descendants, whose love I treasure.

LAURIE McGAW

THE PICTURE

"Mark." No answer. "Mar-aark!" Still no answer. "Avram Itzik!" his mother tried once more, using his full Yiddish name.

"Here I am, Mom — outside, by the car."

"Oh, there you are. What kind of sandwich would you like me to bring today? Peanut butter and jelly or tuna fish?"

"PB and J, Mom. Thanks."

The summer that Mark turned eight was filled with noisy excitement. His family was building a new home! Every day before lunch, he and his parents stopped by to inspect it. What a thrill that was for Mark: The sights and sounds of hammers and saws. The endless fun of exploring rooms without walls.

Once, when Mark took out his tape measure to check the length and width of something, he made a wish for his house to always be this way — not quite done. But then he realized that if that were to happen, he would never be able to move into his bedroom, which he was really looking forward to. It was a large sunny space with a wide picture window facing the front yard. Mark was happy about that because he always liked to see and hear what was going on in the world.

One morning, as he stood near his parents in the unfinished upstairs hallway, he heard his dad say, "And this will be just the right spot for that photograph of my great-grandfather Avram, don't you think?"

"Yes. It will be nice to be able to take that picture out of the closet," Mark's mom said.

"Uh-oh," Mark thought, frowning to himself. "They're going to hang it up!"

Just as Mark was thinking about this problem, his new friend, Ari, came upstairs looking for him. Not only were they soon to be next-door neighbors, but they were going to be in the third grade together that fall.

Happily for Mark, he and Ari had so much to do that day that eventually he completely forgot about the photograph. In fact, he didn't think about it again even once for the rest of the summer.

At last, moving day arrived. As Mark stepped over the threshold, he began his final inspection by ringing the doorbell. It sounded great. And inside, he noticed, all the rooms were cozy and bright, especially his room. Mark loved everything about it — his comfy bed, his desk with the globe, and his dad's telescope, which the two of them looked through every night. But best of all was the empty space right in the middle. It was just large enough for setting up his new train set.

After a few days, Mark decided that his home was perfect in every way — except one. Leaning against the wall outside his room was a picture of a man with a long, gray, scratchy-looking beard and dark, mysterious eyes. It was the photograph of his great-great-grandfather Avram, and Mark didn't like looking at it one bit.

Each morning on his way to breakfast, Mark walked past the picture as swiftly as he could. But every night, after he'd gone to bed, there was no escaping it: That stern-looking man just kept staring at him from the hallway. How Mark wished that his parents would change their minds and put the picture back into the closet.

One day, he tried to hide the picture by covering it with a towel. But when his mother walked by, she simply dusted the frame and took the towel away.

Next, he flipped the picture so that it would face the wall. But when his dad walked by, he just turned it around again.

"It's hopeless," Mark thought as he pulled the covers over his eyes that night. "I'm going to have to live with this scary picture outside my door forever!"

But the following afternoon, something happened to make Mark think that his luck had changed. As usual, when he returned home from school, he ran up the stairs and walked briskly towards his room, carefully avoiding the photograph. This time, though, the hallway seemed different. Slowly, he turned around, faced the wall, and saw . . . nothing! It wasn't there! At first, Mark was so happy. But then he had to wonder: "Where did it go?"

A few moments later, his mother gave him the bad news.

"The framer picked it up this morning. He's going to clean the picture and fix the crack in the frame," she explained. "But don't worry. It will be returned to us soon as good as new, and then we can hang it up on the wall. You know, Mark, someday that picture will belong to you," his mother added with a smile.

"Oh, I'm doomed," he thought, reaching for some apple slices on the counter.

"Hey, honey, not too many. I'm baking with these," his mother said.

"What are you making?" he asked, taking just a few slices.

"An apple cake for our lunch on Rosh Hashanah. It's only two days away, you know!"

"Are Nana and Grandpa Morris coming?"

"Of course. And Nana will be bringing your favorite."

"Honey cake?!" Mark asked.

"Honey cake," his mother answered, laughing.

Mark's eyes widened. "Can Ari come over, too?"

"Actually, I invited his family this morning, and they're going to join us. Isn't that nice?"

"That's great," Mark said, perking up a little. "Mom, about that picture …"

"Sweetheart, excuse me. But can you please bring me the almonds from the pantry?" she asked as she poured the batter into the pan.

"Oh. OK."

"Did you know that that picture is as old as Grandpa Morris?" Mark's mother asked, opening the bag of almonds. "Now, let's see," she said, sprinkling them on top of the batter. "While the apple cake is baking, I can start the challah. Do you want to help me?"

"Sure," Mark said. "Well," he thought, "I guess I'll tell her my idea about moving the picture later, when she isn't so busy. But at least it won't be here to spoil the holiday. Big frames take a long time to fix."

"Isn't it wonderful that Rosh Hashanah comes just in time for the beginning of the school year?" his mother asked. "Everything is new for you: new grade, new books, new teacher — a whole new year!"

Mark agreed. But he couldn't help thinking how much nicer the year would be if they could put a brand new picture in that old wooden frame.

ROSH HASHANAH: A NEW BEGINNING

Mark was practically lifted off the ground and up the steps by a happy group of people entering the synagogue. Squeezing through the crowded doorway, he raced inside ahead of his parents, put on a yarmulke, and found his seat.

"Where's Ari?" Mark wondered, as he looked all around.

Finally, he spotted him walking down the aisle. This was Ari's first Rosh Hashanah in America, and Mark was glad that their families were celebrating it together.

All morning long, Mark enjoyed singing the songs. But there was one thing that he liked even more: the shofar!

"As we are called to hear the sounding of the shofar," the rabbi said, "let us be reminded that we are each responsible for our own actions. Sometimes, we'll have the courage to lead. Other times, we'll have the strength to follow. And still others, it will take all of our courage and all of our strength to stand alone."

When Mark heard the rabbi say *courage*, he immediately thought of Judah the Maccabee, Queen Esther, and Moses. Naturally, he was then reminded of the potato latkes for Chanukah, the hamantashen for Purim, and the egg matzah with strawberry jelly for Passover.

"As usual," Mark thought, "this new year is going to be delicious!"

The loud and joyous sound of the shofar interrupted his daydream. Aaron Stein, who had been B'nai Israel's shofar blower for the past six years, was blowing each note with great care: *tekiah* — one long blast; *shevarim* — three short calls; *teruah* — a series of nine very short notes. The notes were blown over and over again in a certain pattern until finally the last one in the group, the great tekiah — the *tekiah gedolah* — was called out by the rabbi. This one was the most difficult of all because it had to be blown for as long as possible. But somehow, Aaron always managed to thrill everyone. Not surprisingly, he was Mark's hero.

During the two-day celebration of Rosh Hashanah, Mark would hear Aaron blow the shofar a few more times. But once the holiday was over, he wouldn't hear it again until the end of Yom Kippur, ten days away. And even then, it would be blown only once. But what a note it would be — another tekiah gedolah! Mark could hardly wait.

Aaron Stein's record for blowing that note was 46 seconds. How long would he be able to do it this year? Nobody knew. But one thing was certain: As the congregation held its breath with him year in and year out, they were never disappointed. And when he finished, laughter always filled the air as everyone finally exhaled, clapped, and said, "Wow, can you believe he did that!" It was such a joyous way to end the holiday.

Mark hoped that someday he would be able to blow the shofar as well as Aaron. Turning to Ari, he pointed to it and said, "We can do that!"

Ari smiled and nodded, but he didn't look too sure that they really could.

"Shanah Tovah! A happy, healthy new year, Mark," his parents said as they hugged and kissed him at the end of the service.

"Now we have to walk quickly so that our guests don't arrive at our house before we do," his mom said.

Mark and his parents walked so fast that when they got home they still had a little time to relax before lunch. Mark's father was pleased about that because he wanted to get his surprise ready.

When Mark heard the word *surprise*, he begged his dad to tell him what it was.

"You'll see soon enough," his dad said, smiling, as he headed towards the den.

Upstairs in his room, Mark was still wondering what the surprise could be when the doorbell rang. Mark jumped up and looked out his window. It was Nana — with her yummy honey cake — and Grandpa Morris from Baltimore.

"Markeleh!" they cried, as he slid down the banister into their arms.

Mark's grandparents always called him that. That's because they grew up speaking Yiddish. And people who speak Yiddish, they told him, like to add the letters e-l-e-h to the end of a loved one's name as a sign of affection.

Minutes later, the rest of Mark's relatives and Ari and his parents arrived. Standing beside his friend, Mark announced, "Everybody, I'd like you to meet Ari. He used to live in Mexico, but now he lives right next door to me!"

After the introductions were made, everyone followed Mark's mother across the hall as she said, "Let's sit down for lunch, shall we?"

The dining room had never looked like this before!

"It's a wonderland," Mark thought.

The light from the chandelier was making the glasses and the dishes twinkle just like the stars that he and his father gazed at every night. And the holiday food — the matzah ball soup, the noodle kugel, and the sweet potato and apple tsimmes — looked and smelled delicious. But Mark couldn't take his eyes off his favorite, the raisin-filled challah.

Holding it up for all to see, Mark's father explained, "This round challah, which Mark helped to make, by the way, symbolizes an unbroken circle. And a circle represents a whole year."

Then everyone took a slice and topped it with a heaping spoonful of thick golden honey. After they recited the prayer and ate the challah, Mark's father smiled and said, "Now our new year should not only be complete, it should be sweet!"

"If that picture of my great-great-grandfather never comes back from the frame shop, then my new year will be happy, too," Mark thought as he dipped an apple wedge into some honey and took a bite.

During lunch, Grandpa Morris told many stories. Mark particularly liked hearing how his grandfather traveled to school.

Smiling broadly, Grandpa Morris began: "I was lucky because every day, twice a day, I got to skate through the streets of Baltimore."

Mark's father, who had already heard this story, decided that this would be a good time to excuse himself from the table. Grandpa Morris continued: "It was three miles from my home on East Baltimore Street to the Polytechnic Institute, but I did it! Around horses, cars, and buggies, I zigged and I zagged. And I only stopped once — at the bakery, for a sugarcoated bun. Yes, indeed, I was very lucky."

Just as Mark was enjoying a third piece of his nana's honey cake and imagining his grandfather on roller skates, his father returned with a large bundle. It was the surprise! Mark watched as his father and grandfather unwrapped it together. When they untied the string, the paper fell away, and soon everyone was oohing and aahing. But Mark was miserable.

"Oh, no," he moaned to himself. "Not that picture!"

Yet he couldn't let anyone know how he was feeling, especially when he saw what happened next: As Grandpa Morris held it up for a closer look, his smile was so bright that it lit up the face in the picture.

"They actually look happy to see each other!" Mark thought.

"Oh, how I miss my zeyde," Grandpa Morris sighed. "You know, I'll bet that if you were to look up the word *love* in the dictionary, you would find my Grandpa Avram's picture right next to the definition."

"This man?" Mark thought. He couldn't believe what he was hearing.

"You lived with him in Russia when you were a little boy, didn't you," Mark's father said.

"Yes, in our shtetl, our little town, called Aroshka."

Grandpa Morris looked around the sparkling dining room and said, "I remember that we were so poor that the floor in our two-room house was made of clay. And in winter, the only truly warm spot in the house was on a shelf above the wood-burning stove. When I was small, that was my favorite place to sit. You know, everything was different in Aroshka. Even my name! In Russia, my friends called me by my given name, Menashe, or by my nickname, Menashke. Of course, my family went one step further — they always called me Menashkeleh."

"So you're really my Grandpa Menashkeleh?" Mark asked.

"That's right," he said, smiling at his grandson.

"Please tell us about your life in Russia," Mark's father said.

Grandpa Morris closed his eyes for a moment. Then looking at Mark and Ari, he said, "When I was just about your age, my father left our home in Russia to start a better life for us in America. I can still remember the day that I said goodbye to him."

THE GIFT

"Goodbye, Tateh," Morris whispered to his father through his tears. "Menashkeleh, believe me. This will be for the best," Morris's father said softly. "I'll make everything ready for you."

Moments later, Morris's father boarded the train. As Morris watched and waved goodbye, he remembered something amazing that his father had told him: "In America, the stores are like palaces and the streets are paved with gold."

Kicking the dirt beneath his feet, Morris tried to imagine such a beautiful place. He thought of his father working there, helping customers all day. But each evening, when he returned home, there he would be, alone, playing his favorite songs on his violin. This made Morris sad.

So then he pictured himself in this golden land too, rushing into his father's arms to walk home with him at the end of each workday. Now his father wasn't alone anymore.

With the last loud blast of the whistle, the train pulled away and Morris's father began his long, difficult journey. Three uncomfortable train trips, miles and miles of walking, and six bumpy wagon rides later, he would reach the harbor in Bremen, Germany. And there he would board an enormous ship bound for Baltimore in America.

As the train disappeared from sight, Morris wondered how long it would take his father to save enough money to send for the rest of the family. Then, listening to the call of the train's distant whistle, Morris made just one wish: for time to speed by.

But for now, he and his family — his mother, Sarah Mindl; his sister, Freydel; his bubbe, Machlia; and his zeyde, Avram — would go back to Aroshka. Back to one of the dozens of drab wooden houses on one of the many dirt roads that led to the marketplace and the shul in the center of town. Back to Aroshka, to his cousins and friends — Chaikeh, Rebekah, Yosef, Yudis, Devorah, Ruti, and Shai — and to their parents: Herschel, the scribe; Gitel, the baker; Daniel, the carpenter; Sima and Menuchah, the dressmakers; Shmuel, the teacher; Binyamin, the cobbler; Velvel, the peddler; and Efrayim, the shopkeeper.

Back to Aroshka, to live and to wait.

Each weekday was the same as the one before: Morris worked hard in school. Then, after supper, he taught his little sister the names and the sounds of each letter of the Hebrew alphabet.

"This letter is named *shin*," Morris said. "It has a "shuh" sound. The word *shalom*, which means "peace," begins with this letter. Now you try, Freydeleh."

"Shin!" she repeated loudly. "Shalom!" she exclaimed, so fascinated was she by this world of words.

"Very good," Morris said, rubbing his ears.

Grandpa Avram looked up from his book and smiled. "Menashkeleh certainly is a patient teacher," he thought. "And Freydeleh! What an enthusiastic student she is!"

With each passing week, Morris grew to miss his father more and more. But because he had the rest of his family around him, he never felt sad for very long. His mother and his bubbe were as warm as their delicious noodle kugel. And his zeyde, Avram, was as lively as his stories. Indeed, Morris's most happy hours were spent eating noodle kugel while listening to his grandfather.

"Which story shall we hear this afternoon?" Grandpa Avram would ask as he got up from his worktable to join Morris on the bench.

Sometimes, Grandpa Avram made up his own exciting adventures. And other times, he told legends from the Bible. Morris especially liked the one about Joseph and his coat of many colors. Then as soon as Grandpa Avram finished telling a story, it was Morris's turn. How he loved to hear his grandfather laugh at his jokes or ask "What happened next?" whenever he told him a story with a cliffhanger.

"I'll tell you tonight, Zeyde!" Morris would answer, running out the door. Lunch was over. It was time to get back to school.

These were some of Morris's most joyful moments.

But the most sparkling thread in the spindle of life in Aroshka was Shabbat.

To welcome this magical time into their home, Morris's mother, bubbe, and sister drew close to kindle the Shabbos candles. Then, after Grandpa Avram and Morris returned home from shul, the family gathered around the table to hear Grandpa Avram sing the blessings over the wine and the challah. Sometimes, just the five of them would enjoy the special meal of fish, soup, and chicken that followed. But more often than not, Morris and his grandfather would invite a hungry traveler or a poor student to join them. For as Grandpa Avram liked to say, "Sharing Shabbos doubles its sweetness." And he was right.

When morning came, Morris once again accompanied his grandfather to shul. On the way there, Grandpa Avram delighted Morris by answering all of his questions about trees and flowers and clouds, anything and everything that Morris could think of. And as for the rest of the day, it was spent blissfully with family and friends — resting, playing, listening to stories, singing, studying, and enjoying the warm afternoon meal of cholent — meat, potatoes, and beans.

Finally, after the sun had set once more, Grandpa Avram and Morris stepped outside. Looking up, they talked quietly so as not to disturb the sounds of evening while searching for three medium-size stars.

"Is that medium-size, Zeyde?" Morris asked, pointing toward one particular star.

"Yes, I believe you've found a good one, Menashkeleh," Grandpa Avram answered.

"And how about that one over there to the left? Do you see it? Do you think that one is a good match?" Morris asked.

"Perhaps that is a bit too big. We'll see. Let's keep looking," he answered.

One by one they found them, and then, slowly — "Don't rush, Menashkeleh" — walked back inside to tell everyone that Shabbos was over.

The bright flame of the Havdalah candle used during the evening service to separate Shabbat from the new week had been extinguished. And the wine had been blessed. But the sweet smell of the spices would linger in Morris's memory as a reminder of just how perfect the day had been.

"A gute vokh, kinderlakh," Morris's mother and grandparents would say with a hug as the flame went out. "A good week, children."

Always the same wish … in Aroshka.

To Morris, every week was good because he could always look forward to Shabbat. But sprinkled throughout the year came other holidays too, called festivals. Happily for Morris, his Grandpa Avram loved to tell each one's history through stories. Of all of them, Morris's favorite was the one about Chanukah — the Festival of Lights.

"It was a miracle. A small jar of oil, just enough to light the Temple's menorah for one day, miraculously burned for eight," Grandpa Avram began. Sometimes, he liked to begin his stories at the end.

And one time, for the New Year, Grandpa Avram did something extra-special: He taught Morris how to make music with his voice. For hours Morris practiced, and then suddenly he sounded just like the shofar that was blown at Rosh Hashanah and Yom Kippur. Hearing his grandson do it so well made Avram beam with pride. Someday, he knew, Morris would be old enough to learn how to blow a real shofar. And he looked forward to the day that he could begin teaching him.

Three years passed by slowly. And even though Morris didn't always have enough to eat, even though the house was too small, and even though his father was thousands of miles away from him, Morris was happy in Aroshka for one reason: there was always enough love.

Then, one month before Morris's tenth birthday, the family received a letter from Morris's father. Tucked inside were the tickets for their journey to America.

The day before they were to leave, while the family was packing, Grandpa Avram found a quiet moment to talk with Morris.

"My dear Menashkeleh," he said, taking the shofar down from the shelf and gently placing it in his grandson's hands. "This belonged to my grandfather, and now it belongs to you."

"Zeyde, your shofar? You're giving this to me? Really? But it's your treasure."

"No, Menashkeleh, you are my treasure. And it would make me happy if you would keep this with you always. Also, I want you to promise me something. Promise me that you'll keep up with your practicing. You know, you are becoming such a strong shofar blower that one day, I'm sure, I'll close my eyes in shul to listen and it will be you that I hear."

Morris wrapped his hands around the shofar and tried not to cry.

TO AMERICA

As Grandpa Avram lifted the bundles and the basket and loaded them slowly into the wagon, Morris said farewell to his family's relatives and friends. "Gey gezunterheyt!" they all said. "Go in good health!"

In the horse-drawn wagon, with Avram at the reins, Morris sat between his grandparents. His mother and his sister huddled closely in the back. It was a long way to the train station, but the cold autumn wind that was whipping in Morris's face made him feel that the trip would never end. Snuggled under a blanket with his bubbe's arm around him, he almost wished that it wouldn't. Of course, he was excited about going to America, but he was also sad about leaving his grandparents behind.

When they finally arrived at the station, the train was still not due for a half hour, so Morris held onto his sister's hand until it was time to go. His mother sat between her parents on an old wooden bench in front of the track. Sitting arm-in-arm, they pulled

each other close and talked and hugged and kissed. And cried.

Once aboard the train, Morris looked out the window. He saw his grandmother leaning on the bench, wiping her eyes with a handkerchief. He tried to smile at her, to make her smile, but he couldn't.

Earlier, before he boarded the train, he had hugged his grandparents with all his might and had promised to take good care of his mother and his little sister. Now he wished that he could take care of his bubbe, too, and dry her tears. But he couldn't even stop his own.

Suddenly, the train lurched forward and started down the track. Grandpa Avram, who had been holding Morris's hand and talking to him through the open window, now walked alongside the slow-moving train.

"Oh, Menashkeleh," Grandpa Avram said, "nothing can ever truly part us. Each day when we look up into the sky, we'll see the same moon and the same sun and the same stars."

"I'll love you forever, Zeyde!"

"Yes, forever, Menashkeleh! Gedenk!" he answered, wiping away the tears that were streaming down his grandson's face and his own. "Remember!"

"I'll remember!" Morris cried.

Much too soon, the train began to pull away faster and faster, forcing them to let go of each other's hands. In that instant, Grandpa Avram reached out farther for Morris, and Morris stretched out his hand towards his grandfather, but the train was moving much too quickly now. They could only hold onto each other for a few minutes more with their eyes. And Morris held on as long as he could, for he knew that he would never see his grandfather again.

* * *

When Grandpa Morris finished telling the story, he wiped away a tear and said, "Even though I was just a little boy when I lived with my grandparents, I have never forgotten their love."

Everyone was quiet. After a few moments, Mark's father asked Grandpa Morris if he would talk about his voyage to America.

"Ah, the trip across the Atlantic Ocean," he replied with a gleam in his eyes. "Do you really want to hear all this?" he asked.

Everyone said, "Yes, please!"

"Well, it was early in November when we set sail from Bremen, Germany. Two thousand people on one ship! Can you imagine? Russians, Poles, Lithuanians, Hungarians, Romanians — all going to the same place: America. As happy as my family was to rejoin my father, it broke our hearts to leave. On the other hand, we really didn't have a choice. Although we had tried to make the best of our lives, life in Aroshka wasn't always easy or secure. Still, once aboard the ship, we wondered, 'Would our new life in a different land really be better than the one we had had in Russia? Would it be hard to learn the language? What would the people be like?' And of course, all the while that we were thinking about ourselves, we never stopped worrying about our family and friends."

"What about the trip, Dad?" Mark's father asked. "Did you stay well? It must have been freezing on the ocean in November."

Grandpa Morris took a sip of his hot tea and then answered: "Well, I didn't catch cold. But I did feel seasick a lot. Sometimes, though, when the ocean wasn't rough, my sister and I would come up from the cramped decks below to play and get some air. And on those days, I loved the ocean. But do you know what was even worse than the seasickness?" Grandpa Morris said, pausing to take a bite of honey cake. "The food. It was horrible! Every day, we were served the same thing: salty fish — herring. All in all, I couldn't recommend traveling this way. Anyway, after fourteen days at sea, we finally pulled into Baltimore harbor. I can still remember the feeling that I had when I walked off the ship. I was so anxious. For somewhere, I knew, in the crowd of people waiting on the pier below was my father! But before we could see him, we had to file into a building to answer many, many questions and go through even more medical inspections. Apparently, the one that we'd had on the ship hadn't been thorough enough. That was difficult. But we did it. We passed. And then we gathered our things and walked out into a beautiful, brisk fall day and into my father's waiting arms. What a wonderful homecoming that was — all smiles, hugs, kisses, and tears. I'll never forget it."

Piercing a wedge of fruit from his plate and holding it slightly aloft, Grandpa Morris continued: "Did you know that when we were reunited on the pier that day, my father gave me something that I had never seen before. It was an orange. And was it delicious! To this day, oranges are my favorite."

"Mine, too!" Mark said. "Grandpa? Did you have to go to school right away when you came to America?"

"Yes. And I didn't know how to speak a word of English! At first, I had no idea what my teacher or my classmates were saying. Hand signals helped a little bit. But after a while, I learned. You see, my mother was an excellent baker," Morris explained. "So children would always be at our house enjoying the cookies and cakes that she had made while we were at school. And the more time I spent with my new friends, the faster I learned the language."

"Excuse me for interrupting," Mark's mother said, "but speaking of cookies and cakes, we have more if anyone has room!"

Even though everyone was satisfied, they all laughed and answered, "Why not!"

Teacups were filled again and again as Grandpa Morris told more stories about his new full life in America.

And Mark, who was now making his way through a fifth piece of his nana's honey cake, hoped this day would never end.

BEYOND THE STARS

Later that afternoon, heading towards his bedroom, Mark noticed that the picture of Avram was back in its usual place. But this time, he wasn't afraid.

Studying the photograph, Mark thought to himself, "Maybe he was just tired. Maybe the day that the picture was taken, he'd been busy making clothes and playing with his grandchildren." Then he tried to imagine the way that Avram was when Grandpa Morris lived with him — full of stories and laughter. He thought of the Shabbos mornings they shared, walking to shul and talking about the world. He pictured him working at his sewing machine, too. And then he saw him holding his grandson's hand for the very last time as the train pulled out of the station so many years ago.

After dinner, Mark's father said, "You know, it's getting late. So tonight, instead of looking at the stars, could you help me hang the picture of Grandpa Avram on the wall?"

"OK. But Dad, if we do it fast, then can we still maybe use the telescope?"

"Sure."

"Oh, and Dad, umm, could you please bring him to my room? I don't think he should be alone there in the hallway."

"I think that can be arranged," his father answered with a smile.

That night, as Mark laid his head on his pillow, he looked up and whispered, "Hi, my name is Mark, and I'm your great-great-grandson. So you can call me Markeleh."

"Now," Mark thought as he drifted off to sleep, "our home is big enough for the whole family."

The next day, after synagogue, Ari came over to practice blowing the shofar with Mark. With Ari's watch in hand, they each took turns timing each other. So far, Ari's best time was three seconds and Mark's best time was five seconds. After a little while, they both grew tired of trying to blast a long note from the shofar, so Mark suggested, "Why don't we make shofar sounds with our voices, the way my Grandpa Morris taught us to do it!"

"That's a great idea," Ari said.

And soon, Mark could hold the note for ten seconds.

Every day that week, Mark's time got better and better and his voice got louder and louder until eventually everyone in the neighborhood agreed that he sounded just like a real shofar.

At last it was time for Yom Kippur. Songs and prayers from a thousand voices filled the sanctuary on Kol Nidre night and all throughout the next day. Then, about a half hour after the sun had slipped below the horizon, Mark got to see what he'd been waiting for: Aaron Stein was walking up the steps to the bimah.

Turning to Ari, Mark whispered, "You know what? Someday I'm going to announce the end of the High Holy Days by blowing the shofar just the way Aaron does."

Standing beside his best friend, Ari smiled, pointed to his watch, and said, "And I'll time you."

On the way home, Mark played the closing moments of Yom Kippur over and over again in his mind: Aaron Stein had done it. He had broken his record by blowing the shofar for 50 seconds!

As Mark thought about how incredible that was, he took in a deep breath, let it all out slowly, and then said, "Mom, Dad, will I ever be a strong shofar blower like Aaron Stein?"

"Of course you will."

Mark wondered about that for a minute, and then he asked, "How far is Baltimore from here?"

"Oh, about 45 minutes. Why?" his dad asked.

"Well, I was thinking. Maybe we could go there every week so Grandpa Morris could give me lessons? Could we?"

Mark's mother and father looked at each other and then turned to him and smiled: "That's a wonderful idea, honey."

Later that evening, Ari came over to play. As the train went round and round, the sound of the shofar filled Mark's imagination once more. But this time, he was the one holding the note for 50 seconds.

"Someday," Mark thought, "I'll do it."

The years passed, Mark held onto his dream by practicing and practicing, and then, one day, it happened.

Mark had just turned thirteen. It was the week after his bar mitzvah when he learned that Aaron Stein was not going to be available to blow the shofar on Yom Kippur.

"Will you be ready to step in?" his rabbi asked.

Mark couldn't believe his ears.

"Yes, I'll be ready! I'm sure I can do it!" he answered.

That was a summer to remember: first his bar mitzvah and then days and nights of perfecting that one glorious note.

The air grew cooler and school began once more, but Mark's mind was on only one goal.

While everyone was walking to shul that bright Yom Kippur morning, Grandpa Morris suddenly stopped to remind the family of something important: "Tonight will be the first time that my Grandpa Avram's shofar will be blown in a synagogue in America!"

Mark's father walked the rest of the way to shul with his arm around his dad.

Throughout the day, Mark held onto the shofar, just thinking. He thought about the hours that his grandfather had spent teaching him, the way that his nana and his parents had encouraged him and had never complained about the noise, and how Ari, his best friend, had always cheered him on.

And now they were all there, smiling at him.

"This is the moment you've been working for, Markeleh," Grandpa Morris said, squeezing his hand.

"Oh, thanks for everything, Grandpa. I wouldn't be here without you."

Standing on the bimah, Mark noticed that the atmosphere was just as he had always imagined it would be. He could actually feel the excitement of the congregation around him.

Then, the rabbi nodded.

Wrapping his hands tightly around the shofar, Mark lifted it towards the ceiling and filled his lungs with air.

"Te...ki...ah ge...dol...aaaa...ah," the rabbi sang.

And the blast was clear and strong.

Blowing the shofar with all his might, Mark watched as the long, twisting note swirled about the room, squeezed through

the double doors, and sailed on to the sky. He felt then that everyone could hear it. No, not just the people in the sanctuary, but everyone — around the world and behind the moon and beyond the stars ... to another place and time ... to the very spot where his shofar came from, where his great-great-grandpa Avram sat, with his eyes tightly shut, in the synagogue, listening to his favorite sound.

AFTERWORD

The shofar blower in this story is based upon a real person named Gary Stein. Thirty years ago, when Gary was studying to become a bar mitzvah, he heard that his shul, B'nai Israel Congregation, was looking for young people to participate in the service. Gary decided to volunteer. A student of the trumpet, he thought it would be fun to learn how to blow the shofar. And with Cantor Jacob Friedman's help, he did.

About fifteen years into his career as our shofar blower on Rosh Hashanah, Gary began sounding the shofar at

Gary Stein, blowing the shofar at B'nai Israel Congregation in Rockville, Maryland

the end of Yom Kippur as well. As described in the book, this portion of the service is truly magical. But it isn't easy to blow that note. So here are some helpful tips from Gary to keep in mind:

Before you begin, find a spot to stare at. No matter what's going on around you — no matter how many children are sitting at your feet, tugging at you — you must have complete concentration; otherwise, you won't be able to hear the note when it's called out. Once you have absolute concentration, you will be ready to take a deep breath — a very deep breath. Next, position the end of the shofar at the center of your mouth. (Some people are more comfortable blowing it from the side of the mouth.) Your lips will be pressed tightly against it and your tongue will be pressed out between your teeth at the edge of the opening of the shofar. It's from this position that you will blow air into the shofar. As you do so, remember to pace yourself. Start by blowing softly so that as time goes on you'll have enough breath to finish. And be sure to maintain your mouth's position so that all your breath goes into the shofar.

Does Gary ever fear that only air, rather than sound, will come out? No. And that's because he has confidence. And how does he gain such confidence? By practicing! By the way, each time you finish, you will probably notice a crease down the middle of your mouth from having pressed the edge of the shofar so hard against it. That's normal. It happens to Gary every time.

Our High Holiday hero, Gary Stein is cherished by all those who have listened in awe to the commanding call of his shofar. He and his shofar, which once belonged to his teacher and friend, Cantor Friedman *zt"l*, are a very special part of our services. And no matter where he is, come Rosh Hashanah and Yom Kippur, Gary is always with us. Even when he was away at college, his parents arranged for him to fly home for Rosh Hashanah. He was happy to make the journey because he knew how much it meant to everyone — especially to his father, Marvin Stein, of blessed memory — to hear him blow the shofar. And by then, it had come to mean as much to him as well.

You, too, can become an important part of your synagogue's tradition. One of the best ways to learn how to blow a shofar is to get lessons from a shofar blower in your community. And should you decide to buy a shofar, have someone in the store demonstrate different ones for you. (You'll often find a nice selection of shofars in Jewish gift stores.) Each shofar has its own sound, so take your time as you search for the one that has a sound that is most appealing to you.

Perhaps your family has a photograph or an object that comes from another time and place. Why not use that as a springboard for exploring your family's roots: Interview relatives, identify people in old photo albums, have a family reunion. You'll be amazed at the treasures that await you!

Glossary

H = Hebrew; Y = Yiddish.

Avram: (Y) Pronounced AHV-rum. (The *ah* in *ahv* is pronounced like the *o* in *bother*.)

Aroshka: Pronounced eh-RUSH-keh.*

bimah: (H) The raised platform from which part or all of the service is led, the Torah is read, and the shofar is blown. Pronounced bi-MAH. (The *i* in *bi* is pronounced like the *ee* in *bee*.)

bubbe: (Y) Grandmother. Pronounced BUB-beh.* (The *u* in *bub* is pronounced like the *u* in *put*.) The Americanized version is pronounced BUH-bee, which rhymes with *cubby*.

challah: (H) A braided egg bread. In Hebrew, it's pronounced khah-LAH. In Yiddish, it's pronounced KHAHL-leh.* **

Chanukah, Hannukah: (H) Dedication. Also called the Festival of Lights, it is an eight-day celebration that commemorates the rededication of the Temple following the victory in 165 B.C.E. of the Maccabees over the the Syrians, who had taken possession of the Temple and desecrated it. In Hebrew, it's pronounced khah-noo-KAH. In Yiddish, it's pronounced KHON-eh-keh.* **

cholent: (Y) A warm Sabbath dish of meat, potatoes, and beans. Pronounced CHOH-lent. (Pronounce the *o* in *choh* like the *o* in *hot*.)*

Freydel(eh): (Y) Pronounced FREY-d'l-(eh).* (Pronounce the *ey* in *frey* like the *ey* in *grey*. The apostrophe stands for a quick *uh* sound between the *d* and the *l*.)

gey gezunterheyt: (Y) Go in good health. Pronounced gey ge-zunt-er-HEYT. (Pronounce the *ey* in *gey* and *heyt* like the *ey* in *grey*; pronounce the *e* in *ge* and *er* like the *e* in *bet*.)

gedenk: (Y) Remember. Pronounced ge-DENK. (Pronounce the *e* in *ge* and *denk* like the *e* in *bet*.)

gedolah: (H) Great, big. Pronounced ge-do-LAH. *(Do* rhymes with *low*.)*

gute vokh: (Y) Good week. Pronounced gut vokh.** (Pronounce the *u* in *gut* like the *u* in *put*; pronounce the *o* in *vokh* like the *a* in *ball*.)

hamantash (singular), **hamantashen** (plural): (Y) Triangular pastries filled with fruit or poppy seeds. The singular form is pronounced HAW-men-tosh. The plural form is pronounced HAW-men-TOSH'n. *(Tosh* rhymes with *nosh*. The apostrophe stands for a quick *ih* sound between the *sh* and the *n*.)*

Havdalah: (H) Separation. The ceremony that marks the end of the Sabbath or a holy day. Pronounced hav-da-LAH. (Pronounce the *a* in *hav* and *da* as *ah*.)

kinderlakh: (Y) Little children. Pronounced KIN-der-lahkh. (Pronounce the *e* in *der* like the *e* in *bet*.)**

kugel: (Y) A baked casserole of noodles or potatoes, with raisins or prunes or apples or nuts or cottage cheese. Pronounced KU-g'l. (Pronounce the *u* in *ku* like the *oo* in *good*. The apostrophe stands for a quick *uh* sound between the *g* and the *l*.)

latke (singular), **latkes** (plural): (Y) Potato pancake(s). Pronounced LOT-keh, LOT-kehz.*

Machlia: (Y) Pronounced MAKH-lee-eh.* **

Markeleh: (Y) An affectionate nickname for *Mark*. Pronounced MARK-eh-leh.*

matzah: (H) Unleavened bread. In Hebrew, it's pronounced ma-TSAH. (Pronounce the *ts* in *tsah* like the *ts* sound in *bits*.) In Yiddish, it's MOTT-seh. The plural is MOTT-sehz.*

Menashkeleh: (Y) Pronounced meh-NOSH-keh-leh. It is an affectionate nickname for *Menashke* (pronounced meh-NOSH-keh), which itself is the nickname for *Menashe* (pronounced meh-NOSH-eh).*

menorah: (H) Candelabrum. Pronounced m'no-RAH. (The apostrophe stands for a quick *eh* sound between the *m* and the *n*.) In Yiddish, it's pronounced men-AW-ra.

Rosh Hashanah: (H) The Jewish New Year. In Hebrew, it's pronounced rosh ha-sha-NAH.

Sarah Mindl: (Y) Pronounced SAWR-ah MIN-d'l.

Shabbat (H), **Shabbos** or **Shabes** or **Shabbes** (Y): These are the Hebrew and Yiddish forms for *Sabbath*. Pronounced shah-BAHT and SHAH-biss, respectively.

Shanah Tovah: (H) Literally, good (tovah) year (shanah). A greeting that means "Happy New Year." Pronounced sha-NAH to-VAH. (*To* rhymes with *low*.)

shevarim: (H) A shofar note. Pronounced sheh-va-RIM. (The *i* in *rim* is pronounced like the *ee* in *bee*.)

shofar: (H) A trumpet made from a ram's horn. It is blown during Rosh Hashanah, at the end of Yom Kippur, and on special occasions, such as the inauguration of the president (in Israel) and at groundbreaking ceremonies for synagogues. In Hebrew, it's pronounced show-FAR. In Yiddish, it's pronounced SHOW-fur.

shtetl: (Y) A small and wholly (or predominantly) Jewish town in Eastern Europe. Pronounced SHTEH-t'l. (The apostrophe stands for a quick *uh* sound between the *t* and the *l*.) Plural: shtetls or shtetlakh.**

shul: (Y) Synagogue. Rhymes with *full*.

tateh: (Y) Dad, papa. Pronounced TAH-teh.*

tekiah: (H) A shofar note. Pronounced te-ki-AH. (The *e* in *te* is pronounced like the *i* in *it*. The *i* in *ki* is pronounced like the *ee* in *bee*.)

teruah: (H) A shofar note. Pronounced t'ru-AH.

tsimmes: (Y) A baked casserole of carrots, sweet potatoes, and dried fruit, such as raisins. Pronounced TSI-mess.* (Pronounce the *ts* in *tsi* like the *ts* sound in *bits*.)

yarmulke: (Y) Skullcap. Pronounced YAHR-m'l-keh. The Americanized version is pronounced YAH-meh-keh.*

Yom Kippur: (H) The Day of Atonement. In Hebrew, it's pronounced yome ki-POOR. (The *i* in *ki* is pronounced like the *ee* in *bee*.)

zeyde, zayde: (Y) Grandfather. Pronounced ZAY-deh.* The Americanized version is pronounced ZAY-dee.

zt"l: (H) These letters stand for *zekher tsaddik livrakha*. Pronounced zeh-KHAIR tsa-DIK liv-rah-KHA. It means "May the memory of the pious be for a blessing." (Pronounce the *ts* in *tsa* like the *ts* sound in *bits*, the *i* in *dik* like the *ee* in *bee*, and the *i* in *liv* like the *i* in *it*.)**

* For Yiddish words: Pronounce the *e* in *beh, deh, eh, ess, keh, kehz, leh, lent, meh, seh, sehz,* and *teh* like the first and last *a* in *banana*.

** Pronounce *kh* like the *ch* sound in *Bach*.

Pronounce these names from p. 22 as follows: Chaikeh: KHAY-keh (pronounce *ay* in *khay* like the *y* in *my*); Menuchah: m'NU-kha; Shmuel: SHMU'l; Shai: SHAY (pronounce *ay* in *shay* like the *y* in *my*); Sima: SI-mah (pronounce *i* in *si* like *ee* in *bee*).* **

Author's Acknowledgments

To my wonderful family — my parents, Herschel and Goldene Blumberg; Jim Catler; Susan B. Levin; Mark Blumberg; Josephine McCarty; Aaron Levin; and Ari Levin: Deepest thanks for your constant love and encouragement, for your inspiration, and for your excellent suggestions!

To my other treasured relatives and friends, thank you for your affection and unwavering support.

Heartfelt gratitude to Ellen E. M. Roberts (Where Books Begin, New York) and Kirsten Neuhaus for your friendship and your extraordinary vision.

Special thanks to the following for taking the time to read the manuscript. Your comments were invaluable: Rabbi Matthew Simon, Sara Rubinow Simon, Rabbi Jonathan Schnitzer, Naomi Morse, Fran Starr Berger Kahn, Leora Starr Kahn, Paul Frieden, Janet Weissman, Carol Minkoff, Vanessa Constantine, and Charles Patterson.

Much appreciation also to Rose Coplon, Cantor Deborah Togut, Bilha Marcus, Herman Taube, and Joshua Youlus for your helpfulness with Hebrew and Yiddish; Menachem Youlus, for your guidance in choosing a shofar; Yeshaya Metal (Librarian, YIVO Institute for Jewish Research), for answering my questions; Gary Stein, for sharing the art of blowing the shofar and for that fantastic photograph in the Afterword; and Robin Waldman (Lloyd Street Museum, Baltimore, Maryland), Andrew Ausseon (PhotoAssist), and Chris Piercy (The Baltimore Polytechnic Institute Foundation, Inc.), for your kindness and photo research assistance.

To all the special people who modeled, I am forever beholden to you for your warmth and your enthusiasm for bringing this story to life.

To Andrew Smith, of PageWave Graphics, I am grateful for your charming disposition, your humor, and your masterly design work.

And finally, to my friend Laurie McGaw: Your magnificent illustrations are just as I dreamed they would be. Thank you for taking this journey with me and for making each step along the way such a joy!

MARGIE BLUMBERG

Illustrator's Acknowledgments

To my husband, Ross Phillips: You are my most trusted critic and loving partner in every adventure. Thank you. To our children, Gwynne and Owen: Thanks for your valuable observations and hugs. To my mother-in-law, Kathleen Phillips: Thank you for your love and encouragement and for Avram's antique frame. And to my parents, Ted and Carol McGaw, and my brother, Rob: The memory of their love is always an inspiration to me.

From the beginning, my right-hand gal was Linda Kabot: Thank you for helping with absolutely everything.

Warmest thanks go to all the people who modeled for this book, new friends and old. I am deeply grateful. The cast of characters: Gavin Ockrant (Mark); Cheryl Green-Ockrant and Bernie Ockrant (Mark's parents); Cubby Marcus (Avram); Tanya Kadin (Machlia); Charles Kadin (Grandpa Morris); Linda Kabot (Nana); Matty Goldman (young Morris); Linda Goldman (Sarah Mindl); Rachel Bain (Freydel); Matthew Himmel (Ari); Wendy and Stuart Himmel (Ari's parents); Matthew Ockrant (roller-skating Morris); Rabbi Philip S. Scheim and Cantor Marshall Loomer (the rabbi and the cantor in the synagogue scenes); Evan Shapiro (shofar blower); Paul Cash (Morris's father, Benjamin); and Joel Goldman (the butcher in the roller-skating scene).

Many thanks also to the following models who appear in various scenes: Randy, Garry, Shawn, Jared, and Hartley Shapiro; Jordan and Bradley Ockrant; Debbie and Melissa Cash; Rhona, Bruce, Robbie, and Hannah Wulfsohn; Sara, Neil, and Dylan Smibert; Michael Himmel; Sarah, Clare, and James Scott; Stan, Heather, Blair, Jordana, and Lauren Mincer; and Jillian Levick.

Special thanks go to Rabbi Philip S. Scheim and Cantor Marshall Loomer for the photo session at Beth David B'nai Israel Beth Am Synagogue in Toronto, and to Vivian Kellner and Sharon O'Brien, whose assistance that day was most appreciated.

Much gratitude to Cathy Goldman, Jaime Goldman, Jack Kabot, Lorna and Larry Bain and family, Eva Blaff and Jeff Nemers and family, and Tova Rosenberg, principal of the United Synagogue Day School in Richmond Hill.

Thanks to Jonathan Freedman, Rona Abramovitch, and Jacob Freedman for your love and support. Many thanks to Eric Smith, engineer at the South Simcoe Railway in Tottenham, Ontario. To book designer extraordinaire, Andrew Smith: Thank you for your patient and good-natured guidance throughout this project.

And finally, to Margie Blumberg: It has been such a pleasure working closely with someone who really "sees." You were my second set of eyes. I've enjoyed learning more about Jewish culture. But mostly, I value our friendship.

LAURIE McGAW